PU

FANTASTIC STORIES

Terry Jones was born in 1942 in Wales. He read English at Oxford University and retains a passion for medieval history and literature: his study of Chaucer's Knight received wide critical acclaim when it was published some years ago. He became well known to the general public as a member of the Monty Python team. He co-directed *Monty Python and the Holy Grail* and directed *Monty Python's Life of Brian* (which won the Grand Jury prize at Cannes in 1983), *Eric the Viking, Personal Services* and *The Wind in the Willows* (which won the Best Film in the International Children's Film Festival in Chicago in 1998).

Terry Jones is married and lives in London.

Other books by Terry Jones

FAIRY TALES
THE KNIGHT AND THE SQUIRE
THE LADY AND THE SQUIRE
NICOBOBINUS
THE SAGA OF ERIK THE VIKING

Terry Jones

FANTASTIC STORIES

Illustrated by Michael Foreman

PUFFIN BOOKS

PUFFIN BOOKS

Published by the Penguin Group
Penguin Books Ltd, 80 Strand, London WC2R 0RL, England
Penguin Putnam Inc., 375 Hudson Street, New York, New York 10014, USA
Penguin Books Australia Ltd, 250 Camberwell Road, Camberwell, Victoria 3124, Australia
Penguin Books Canada Ltd, 10 Alcorn Avenue, Toronto, Ontario, Canada M4V 3B2
Penguin Books India (P) Ltd, 11 Community Centre, Panchsheel Park,
New Delhi – 110 017, India
Penguin Books (NZ) Ltd, Cnr Rosedale and Airborne Roads,
Albany, Auckland, New Zealand
Penguin Books (South Africa) (Pty) Ltd, 24 Sturdee Avenue, Rosebank 2196, South Africa

Penguin Books Ltd, Registered Offices: 80 Strand, London WC2R 0RL England

www.penguin.com

First published by Pavilion Books 1992
Published in Puffin Books 1994
Published with black and white illustrations 1995
This edition has been produced exclusively for Nestlé Cheerios and
Honey Nut Cheerios 2003
2

Set in 13/14 pt Monophoto Baskerville

Filmset by Datix International Limited, Bungay, Suffolk
Made and printed in England by Clays Ltd, St Ives plc

British Library Cataloguing in Publication Data
A CIP catalogue record for this book is available from the British Library

ISBN 0-141-31669-1

For Tom Crowley
who heard most of these stories first

To the Reader

Although most of these stories could be called 'Fairy Tales' some of them don't fit that description, so I've named the book *Fantastic Stories*. Most of the tales were written between the end of November 1991 and the middle of January 1992.

I'd also like to thank my son, Bill Jones, for giving me the end of 'The Improving Mirror'.

Terry Jones

Contents

The Ship of Fools ~ 1
The Dragon on the Roof ~ 9
The Star of the Farmyard ~ 22
The Improving Mirror ~ 32
The Mermaid Who Pitied a Sailor ~ 42
Forget-Me-Nuts ~ 48
Eyes-All-Over ~ 62
The Snow Baby ~ 70
How the Badger Got Its Stripes ~ 76

The Ship of Fools

A young boy named Ben once ran away to sea. But the ship he joined was a very odd one indeed.

The Captain always wore his trousers tied over his head with seaweed. The Bosun danced the hornpipe all day long from dawn to dusk wearing nothing but beetroot juice. And the First Mate kept six families of mice down the neck of his jumper!

'This is a rum vessel, me hearty!' said Ben to one of the sailors, who was at that moment about to put his head into the ship's barrel of syrup.

'It's a Ship of Fools!' grinned the sailor, and he stuck his head in the syrup.

'I suppose you all must know what you're doing,' murmured young Ben, but the sailor couldn't reply because he was all stuck up with syrup.

Just then the Captain yelled: 'Raise the hanky! And sit on the snails!' Although, because he still had his trousers over his head, what it actually sounded like was: 'Gmpf der wmfky! Umf bmfwmf umf wmf!'

'I'm sure he means: "Raise the anchor! And set the sails!"' said young Ben to himself. But whatever it was the Captain had said, nobody seemed to be taking the slightest bit of notice.

'They must be doing more important things,' said Ben to himself. 'So I suppose *I'd* better obey Captain's orders.'

So Ben raised the anchor by himself, and hoisted the sails as best he could, and the ship sailed off into the blue.

'Where are we heading, shipmate?' Ben asked a sailor who was hanging over the side, trying to paint the ship with a turnip and a pot of lemonade.

'Goodness knows!' exclaimed the sailor. 'It's a Ship of Fools!'

'The Captain will know,' said Ben, and he climbed up to the bridge, where the Captain was standing upside-down at the wheel, trying to steer with his feet.

'I'm almost sure you shouldn't steer a ship like that,' said Ben to himself, 'but then what do I know? I'm just a raw land-lubber getting his first taste of the briney.' But even so, Ben realized that the Captain couldn't see where they were going, because his trousers were still over his eyes. As it happened, the ship was, at that moment, heading straight for a lighthouse! So Ben grabbed the wheel, and said: 'What's the course, skipper?'

'Bmf Bmf Wmf!' replied the Captain.

'Nor' Nor' West it is, sir!' said Ben, and he steered the ship safely round the lighthouse and off for the open sea.

Well, they hadn't sailed very far before a storm blew up.

'Shall I take in the yard-arm and reef the sails, Captain?' yelled Ben. But the Captain was far too busy trying to keep his game of marbles still, as the ship rolled from side to side.

The wind began to howl, and the sea grew angry.

'I better had, anyway,' said Ben to himself, and he ran about the ship, preparing for the storm ahead.

As he did so, the rest of the crew grinned and waved at him, but they all carried on doing whatever it was they were doing. One of them was hanging by his hair from the mainmast, trying to play the violin with a spoon. Another was varnishing his nose with the ship's varnish. While another was trying to stretch his ears by tying them to the capstan and jumping overboard.

'Well . . . I wouldn't have thought this was the way to run a ship!' said young Ben. 'I suppose they know the ropes and I'm just learning. Even so . . . I didn't realize the newest recruit had to do *everything*! But I suppose I'd better get on with it.' And he set about doing what he thought should be done, while the rest of the crew just grinned and waved at him.

The storm gathered force, and soon great waves

were lashing across the deck, as the ship rolled and wallowed. Ben rushed about trying to get everyone below decks, so he could batten down the hatches. But as soon as he got one sailor to go below another would pop up from somewhere else.

And all the time, the ship rolled, and before long it began to take on water.

'Cap'n! We must get the men below decks and batten down the hatches, while we ride out the storm!' yelled Ben.

But the Captain had decided to take his supper on the fo'c'sle, and was far too busy – trying to keep the waves off his lamb chop with an egg whisk – to listen to Ben.

And still the ship took on more water.

'She's beginning to list!' shouted Ben. 'The hold's filling with water!'

'It's OK!' said the Bosun, who had stopped doing the hornpipe, but was still only wearing beetroot juice. 'Look!' and he held up a large piece of wood.

'What's that?' gasped Ben.

'It's the ship's bung!' said the Bosun proudly. 'Now any water will run out through the bunghole in the bottom of the ship!'

'You're a fool!' yelled Ben.

'I know!' grinned the Bosun. 'It's a Ship of Fools!'

'Now we'll sink for sure!' cried Ben.

And, sure enough, the ship began to sink.

'Man the lifeboats!' yelled Ben. But the fools had all climbed up the mast and were now clinging

to it, playing conkers and 'I Spy With My Little Eye'.

So Ben had to launch the lifeboat on his own. And he only managed to do it just as the ship finally went down. Then he had to paddle around in the terrible seas, fishing the crew of fools out of the heaving waters.

'I spy with my little eye something beginning with . . . S!' shouted the First Mate, as Ben hauled him into the lifeboat.

'Sea,' said Ben wearily, and rowed over to the next fool.

By the time night fell, Ben had managed to get the Captain and the Bosun and the First Mate and all the rest of the crew of fools into the little lifeboat. But they wouldn't keep still, and they kept shouting and laughing and falling overboard again, and Ben had his work cut out trying to keep them all together.

By dawn the storm had died down, and Ben was exhausted, but he'd managed to save everyone. One of the fools, however, had thrown all the oars overboard while Ben hadn't been watching, so they couldn't row anywhere. And now the First Mate was so hungry he'd started to eat the lifeboat!

'You can't eat wood!' yelled Ben.

'You can – if you're fool enough!' grinned the First Mate.

'But if you eat the lifeboat, we'll all drown!' gasped Ben.

'It's a pity we don't have a little pepper and salt,' remarked the Captain, who had also started to nibble the boat.

'It's salty enough as it is!' said the Bosun, who was tucking into the rudder.

'Urgh!' said the Chief Petty Officer. 'It's uncooked! You shouldn't eat raw lifeboat!'

But they did.

By midday, they'd managed to eat most of the lifeboat, and Ben had just given them all up for lost, when, to his relief, he saw land on the horizon.

'Land ahead!' shouted Ben, and he tried to get the fools to paddle with their hands towards it, but they were feeling a bit sick from all the wood they'd just eaten. So Ben broke off the last plank and used that to paddle them towards the shore.

At last they landed, and the fools all jumped ashore and started filling their trousers with sand and banging their heads on the rocks, while young Ben looked for food.

He hadn't looked very far, when a man with a spear suddenly barred his way.

Ben tried to signal that he meant no harm, that he had been shipwrecked, and that he and his crewmates were in sore distress. Once the man understood all this, he became very friendly, and offered Ben food and drink. But as soon as the two of them returned to Ben's shipmates, the crew of fools all leapt up making terrible faces and tried to chase the stranger off.

'Stop it!' cried Ben. 'He's trying to help us!' But the crew of fools had already jumped on the poor fellow, and started beating and punching him, until eventually he fled back to his village to fetch a war party.

'Now we can't even stay here!' screamed Ben. 'You're all fools!'

'Of course we are!' cried the Captain. 'We keep telling you – it's a Ship of Fools!'

Now I don't know how what happened next came about, or what would have happened to Ben if it hadn't, but it did. And this is what it was.

Young Ben was just wondering what on earth he was going to do, when a sail appeared on the horizon!

But before Ben could shout out: 'There's a ship!' he turned and saw the war party approaching with spears and bows and arrows, while the crew of fools were busy trying to bury the Bosun head-first in the sand.

Ben finally shook his head and said: 'Well, you've all certainly taught me one thing: and that's not to waste my time with those I can see are fools – no matter who they are – Captain, Bosun or First Mate!'

And with that, Ben dived into the sea and swam off to join the other boat. And he left the Ship of Fools to their own fate.

The Dragon on the Roof

A long time ago in a remote part of China, a dragon once flew down from the mountains and settled on the roof of the house of a rich merchant.

The merchant and his wife and family and servants were, of course, terrified out of their wits. They looked out of the windows and could see the shadows of the dragon's wings stretching out over the ground below them. And when they looked up, they could see his great yellow claws sticking into the roof above them.

'What are we going to do?' cried the merchant's wife.

'Perhaps it'll be gone in the morning,' said the merchant. 'Let's go to bed and hope.'

So they all went to bed and lay there shivering and shaking. And nobody slept a wink all night. They just lay there listening to the sound of the dragon's leathery wings beating on the walls behind their beds, and the scraping of the dragon's scaly belly on the tiles above their heads.

The next day, the dragon was still there, warming its tail on the chimney-pot. And no one in the house dared to stick so much as a finger out of doors.

'We can't go on like this!' cried the merchant's wife. 'Sometimes dragons stay like that for a thousand years!'

So once again they waited until nightfall, but this time the merchant and his family and servants crept out of the house as quiet as could be. They could hear the dragon snoring away high above them, and they could feel the warm breeze of his breath blowing down their necks, as they tiptoed across the lawns. By the time they got half-way across, they were so frightened that they all suddenly started to run. They ran out of the gardens and off into the night. And they didn't stop running until they'd reached the great city, where the king of that part of China lived.

The next day, the merchant went to the King's palace. Outside the gates was a huge crowd of beggars and poor people and ragged children, and the rich merchant had to fight his way through them.

'What d'you want?' demanded the palace guard.

'I want to see the King,' exclaimed the merchant.

'Buzz off!' said the guard.

'I don't want charity!' replied the merchant. 'I'm a rich man!'

'Oh, then in you go!' said the guard.

So the merchant entered the palace, and found the King playing Fiddlesticks with his Lord High Chancellor in the Council Chamber. The merchant fell on his face in front of the King, and cried: 'O Great King! Favourite Of His People! Help me! The Jade Dragon has flown down from the Jade Dragon Snow Mountain, and has alighted on my roof-top, O Most Beloved Ruler Of All China!'

The King (who was, in fact, extremely unpopular) paused for a moment in his game and looked at the merchant, and said: 'I don't particularly like your hat.'

So the merchant, of course, threw his hat out of the window, and said: 'O Monarch Esteemed By All His Subjects! Loved By All The World! Please assist me and my wretched family! The Jade Dragon has flown down from the Jade Dragon Snow Mountain, and is, at this very moment, sitting on my roof-top, and refuses to go away!'

The King turned again, and glared at the merchant, and said: 'Nor do I much care for your trousers.'

So the merchant, naturally, removed his trousers and threw them out of the window.

'Nor,' said the King, 'do I really approve of anything you are wearing.'

So, of course, the merchant took off all the rest of his clothes, and stood there stark naked in front of the King, feeling very embarrassed.

'*And* throw them out of the window!' said the King.

So the merchant threw them out of the window. At which point, the King burst out into the most unpleasant laughter. 'It must be your birthday!' he cried, 'because you're wearing your birthday suit!' and he collapsed on the floor helpless with mirth. (You can see why he wasn't a very popular king.)

Finally, however, the King pulled himself together and asked: 'Well, what do you want? You can't stand around here stark naked, you know!'

'Your Majesty!' cried the merchant. 'The Jade Dragon has flown down from the Jade Dragon Snow Mountain and is sitting on my roof-top!'

The King went a little green about the gills when he heard this, because nobody particularly likes having a dragon in their kingdom.

'Well, what do you expect me to do about it?' replied the King. 'Go and read it a bedtime story?'

'Oh no! Most Cherished Lord! Admired And Venerated Leader Of His People! No one would expect *you* to read bedtime stories to a dragon. But I was hoping you might find some way of . . . getting rid of it?'

'Is it a big dragon?' asked the King.

'It is. Very big,' replied the merchant.

'I was afraid it would be,' said the King. 'And have you tried asking it – politely – if it would mind leaving of its own accord?'

'First thing we did,' said the merchant.

'Well, in that case,' replied the King, '. . . tough luck!'

Just at that moment there was a terrible noise from outside the palace. 'Ah! It's here!' cried the King, leaping onto a chair. 'The dragon's come to get us!'

'No, no, no,' said the Lord High Chancellor. 'That is nothing to be worried about. It is merely the poor people of your kingdom groaning at your gates, because they have not enough to eat.'

'Miserable wretches!' cried the King. 'Have them all beaten and sent home.'

'Er . . . many of them have no homes to go to,' replied the Chancellor.

'Well then – obviously – just have them beaten!' exclaimed the King. 'And sent somewhere else to groan.'

But just then there was an even louder roar from outside the palace gates.

'*That's* the dragon!' exclaimed the King, hiding in a cupboard.

'No,' said the Chancellor, 'that is merely the rest of your subjects demanding that you resign the crown.'

At this point, the King sat on his throne and burst into tears. 'Why does nobody like me?' he cried.

'Er . . . may I go and put some clothes on?' asked the merchant.

'Oh! Go and jump out of the window!' replied

the King.

Well, the merchant was just going to jump out of the window (because, of course, in those days, whenever a king told you to do something, you always did it) when the Lord High Chancellor stopped him and turned to the King and whispered: 'Your Majesty! It may be that this fellow's dragon could be just what we need!'

'Don't talk piffle,' snapped the King. '*Nobody* needs a dragon!'

'On the contrary,' replied the Chancellor, '*you* need one right now. Nothing, you know, makes a king more popular with his people than getting rid of a dragon for them.'

'You're right!' exclaimed the King.

So there and then he sent for the Most Famous Dragon-Slayer In The Land, and had it announced that a terrible dragon had flown down from the Jade Dragon Snow Mountain and was threatening their kingdom.

Naturally everyone immediately forgot about being hungry or discontented. They fled from the palace gates and hid themselves away in dark corners for fear of the dragon.

Some days later, the Most Famous Dragon-Slayer In The Whole Of China arrived. The King ordered a fabulous banquet in his honour. But the Dragon-Slayer said: 'I never eat so much as a nut, nor drink so much as a thimbleful, until I have seen my dragon, and know what it is I have to do.'

So the merchant took the Dragon-Slayer to his house, and they hid in an apricot tree to observe the dragon.

'Well? What d'you think of it?' asked the merchant.

But the Dragon-Slayer said not a word.

'Big, isn't it?' said the merchant.

But the Dragon-Slayer remained silent. He just sat there in the apricot tree, watching the dragon.

'How are you going to kill it?' inquired the merchant eagerly.

But the Dragon-Slayer didn't reply. He climbed down out of the apricot tree, and returned to the palace. There he ordered a plate of eels and mint, and he drank a cup of wine.

When he had finished, the King looked at him anxiously and said: 'Well? What are you going to do?'

The Dragon-Slayer wiped his mouth and said: 'Nothing.'

'Nothing?' exclaimed the King. 'Is this dragon so big you're frightened of it?'

'I've killed bigger ones,' replied the Dragon-Slayer, rubbing his chest.

'Is it such a fierce dragon you're scared it'll finish you off?' cried the King.

'I've dispatched hundreds of fiercer ones,' yawned the Dragon-Slayer.

'Then has it hotter breath?' demanded the King. 'Or sharper claws? Or bigger jaws? Or what?'

But the Dragon-Slayer merely shut his eyes and

said: 'Like me, it's old and tired. It has come down from the mountains to die in the East. It's merely resting on that roof-top. It'll do no harm, and, in a week or so, it will go on its way to the place where dragons go to die.'

Then the Dragon-Slayer rolled himself up in his cloak and went to sleep by the fire.

But the King was furious.

'This is no good!' he whispered to the Lord High Chancellor. 'It's not going to make me more popular if I leave this dragon sitting on that man's roof-top. It needs to be killed!'

'I agree,' replied the Lord High Chancellor. 'There's nothing like a little dragon-slaying to get the people on to your side.'

So the King sent for the Second Most Famous Dragon-Slayer In The Whole Of China, and said: 'Listen! I want you to kill that dragon, and I won't pay you unless you do!'

So the Second Most Famous Dragon-Slayer In The Whole Of China went to the merchant's house and hid in the apricot tree to observe the dragon. Then he came back to the palace, and ordered a plate of pork and beans, drank a flask of wine, and said to the King: 'It's a messy business killing dragons. The fire from their nostrils burns the countryside, and their blood poisons the land so that nothing will grow for a hundred years. And when you cut them open, the smoke from their bellies covers the sky and blots out the sun.'

But the King said: 'I want that dragon killed. Mess or no mess!'

But the Second Most Famous Dragon-Slayer In The Whole Of China replied: 'Best to leave this one alone. It's old and on its way to die in the East.'

Whereupon the King stamped his foot, and sent for the Third Most Famous Dragon-Slayer In The Whole Of China, and said: 'Kill me that dragon!'

Now the Third Most Famous Dragon-Slayer In The Whole Of China also happened to be the most cunning, and he knew just why it was the King was so keen to have the dragon killed. He also knew that if he killed the dragon, he himself would become the First Dragon-Slayer In The Whole Of China instead of only the Third. So he said to the King: 'Nothing easier, Your Majesty. I'll kill that dragon straightaway.'

Well, he went to the merchant's house, climbed the apricot tree and looked down at the dragon. He could see it was an old one and weary of life, and he congratulated himself on his good luck. But he told the King to have it announced in the market square that the dragon was young and fierce and very dangerous, and that everyone should keep well out of the way until after the battle was over.

When they heard this, of course, the people were even more frightened, and they hurried back to their hiding places and shut their windows and bolted their doors.

Then the Dragon-Slayer shouted down from the apricot tree: 'Wake up, Jade Dragon! For I have come to kill you!'

The Jade Dragon opened a weary eye and said: 'Leave me alone, Dragon-Slayer. I am old and weary of life. I have come down from the Jade Dragon Snow Mountain to die in the East. Why should you kill me?'

'Enough!' cried the Dragon-Slayer. 'If you do not want me to kill you, fly away and never come back.'

The Jade Dragon opened its other weary eye and looked at the Dragon-Slayer. 'Dragon-Slayer! You know I am too weary to fly any further. I have settled here to rest. I shall do no one any harm. Let me be.'

But the Dragon-Slayer didn't reply. He took his bow and he took two arrows, and he let one arrow fly, and it pierced the Jade Dragon in the right eye. The old creature roared in pain, and tried to raise itself up on its legs, but it was too old and weak, and it fell down again on top of the house, crushing one of the walls beneath its weight.

Then the Dragon-Slayer fired his second arrow, and it pierced the Jade Dragon in the left eye, and the old creature roared again and a sheet of fire shot out from its nostrils and set fire to the apricot tree.

But the Dragon-Slayer had leapt out of the tree and on to the back of the blinded beast, as it struggled to its feet, breathing flames through its nostrils and setting fire to the countryside all around.

It flapped its old, leathery wings, trying to fly away, but the Dragon-Slayer was hanging on to the spines on its back, and he drove his long sword deep into the dragon's side. And the Jade Dragon howled, and its claws ripped off the roof of the merchant's house, as it rolled over on its side and its blood gushed out on to the ground.

And everywhere the dragon's blood touched the earth, the plants turned black and withered away.

Then the Dragon-Slayer took his long sword and cut open the old dragon's fiery belly, and a black cloud shot up into the sky and covered the sun.

When the people looked out of their hiding places, they thought the night had fallen, the sky was so black. All around the city they could see the countryside burning, and the air stank with the smell of the dragon's blood. But the King ordered a great banquet to be held in the palace that night, and he paid the Dragon-Slayer half the money he had in his treasury.

And when the people heard that the dragon

had been killed, they cheered and clapped and praised the King because he had saved them from the dragon.

When the merchant and his wife and children returned to their house, however, they found it was just a pile of rubble, and their beautiful lawns and gardens were burnt beyond repair.

And the sun did not shine again in that land all that summer, because of the smoke from the dragon's belly. What is worse, nothing would grow in that kingdom for a hundred years, because the land had been poisoned by the dragon's blood.

But the odd thing is, that although the people were now poorer than they ever had been, and scarcely ever had enough to eat or saw the sun, every time the King went out they cheered him and clapped him and called him: 'King Chong The Dragon-Slayer', and he was, from that time on, the most popular ruler in the whole of China for as long as he reigned and long after.

And the Third Most Famous Dragon-Slayer In The Whole Of China became the First, and people never tired of telling and retelling the story of his fearful fight with the Jade Dragon from the Jade Dragon Snow Mountain.

What do you think of that?

The Star of the Farmyard

There was once a dog who could perform the most amazing tricks. It could stand on its head and bark the Dog's Chorus whilst juggling eight balls on its hind paws and playing the violin with its front paws. That was just one of its tricks.

Another trick it could do was this: it would bite its own tail, then it would roll around the farmyard like a wheel, balancing two long poles on its paws – on top of one of which it was balancing Daisy the Cow and on the other Old Lob the Carthorse – all the while, at the same time, telling excruciatingly funny jokes that it made up on the spot.

One day Charlemagne, the cock, said to Stanislav the dog: 'Stan, you're wasted doing your amazing tricks here in this old farmyard – you ought to go to the Big City or join the circus.'

Stan replied: 'Maybe you're right, Charlemagne.'

So one bright spring morning, Stanislav the Dog and Charlemagne the Cock set off down the road to seek their fortunes in the Big City.

They hadn't gone very far before they came to a fair. There were people selling everything you could imagine. There was also a stage on which a troupe of strolling players were performing.

So Charlemagne the Cock strode up to the leader of the troupe and said: 'Now, my good man, this is indeed your lucky day, for you see before you the most talented, most amazing juggler, acrobat, ventriloquist, comedian and all-round entertainer in the whole history of our – or any other – farmyard . . . Stanislav the Dog!' And Stanislav who all this time had been looking modestly down at his paws, now gave a low bow.

'Can't you read?' said the leader of the troupe. 'No dogs!'

And without more ado, Charlemagne the Cock and Stanislav the Dog were thrown out.

'Huh!' said Charlemagne, picking himself up and shaking the road-dust out of his feathers. 'You're too good for a troupe of strolling players anyway.'

Stanislav climbed wearily out of the ditch. He was covered in mud, and he looked at his friend very miserably.

'I'm tired,' he said. And I want to go home to my master.'

'Cheer up, my friend!' replied Charlemagne the Cock. 'We're going to the Big City, where fine ladies and gentlemen drip with diamonds, where dukes and earls sport rubies and emeralds, and where the streets are paved with gold. With your talents, you'll take 'em by storm. We'll make our fortunes!'

So the cock and the dog set off once more down the long, dirty road that led to the Big City.

On the way they happened to pass a circus. Charlemagne the Cock strode up to the ringmaster, who was in the middle of teaching the lions to stand on their hind legs and jump through a ring.

'Tut! tut! tut! my good man,' said Charlemagne the Cock. 'You needn't bother yourself with this sort of rubbish any more! Allow me to introduce you to the most superlative acrobat and tumbler – who can not only stand on his hind paws, but can jump through fifty such rings . . . backwards and whilst balancing one of your lions on his nose . . . and do it all on the high wire . . . *without a safety net*!'

'I only do tricks with lions,' said the ringmaster.

'But Stanislav the Dog has more talent in his right hind leg than your entire troupe of lions!'

'These are the best lions in the business!' exclaimed the ringmaster. 'And they'd eat you and your dog for supper without even blinking. In fact they need a feed right now!' And he reached out his hand to grab Charlemagne the Cock. Stan the Dog saw what was happening, however, and nipped the ringmaster on the ankle.

'Run, Charlemagne!' he yelled.

And Charlemagne ran as fast as he could, while Stan the Dog leapt about – nipping people's ankles

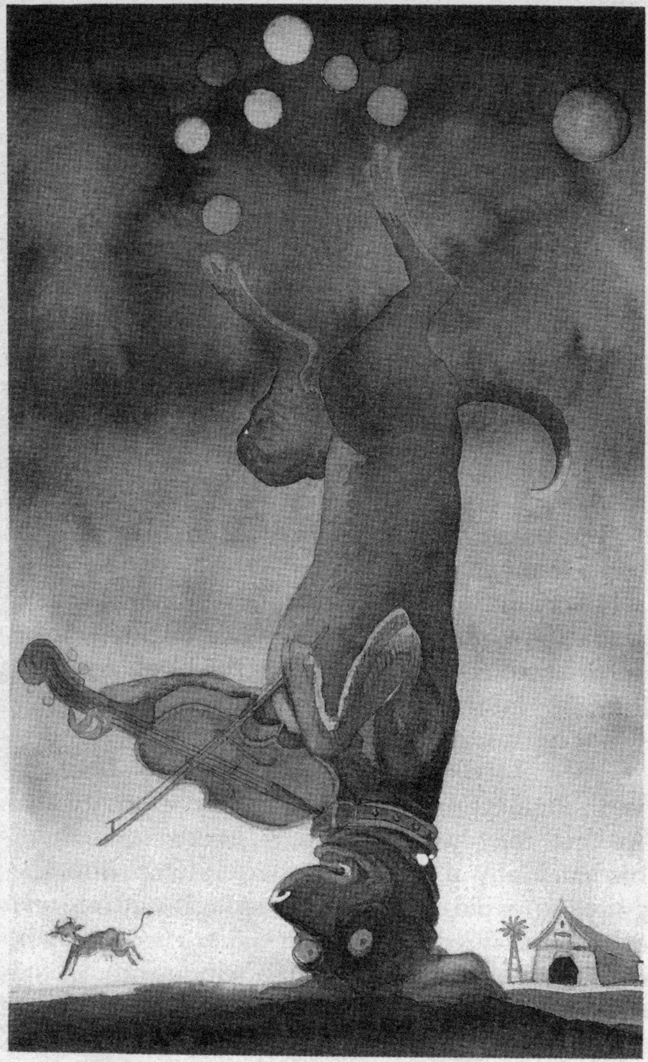

– as the entire circus chased them down the road.

'Help!' squawked Charlemagne, as the circus folk got closer and closer and hands reached out to grab him by the neck.

But Stan the Dog ran under everyone's legs and tripped them up. Then he said to Charlemagne: 'Jump on my back! I can run four times as fast as these clowns!'

And so they escaped, with Charlemagne the Cock riding on Stan the Dog's back.

That night they slept under a hedge. Charlemagne the Cock was extremely nervous, but Stan the Dog curled himself around his friend to protect him. Stan himself, however, was not very happy either.

'I'm hungry,' he murmured, 'and I want to go home to my master.'

'Cheer up!' said Charlemagne. 'Tomorrow we'll reach the Great City, where your talents will be appreciated. Forget these country yokels. I'm telling you – fame and fortune await you and . . .'

But his friend was fast asleep.

Well, the next day, they arrived in the Great City. At first they were overawed by the noise and bustle. Many a time they had to leap into the gutter to avoid a cart or a carriage, and on one occasion they both got drenched when somebody emptied a chamber-pot from a window above the street, and it went right over them.

'Oh dear, I miss the farmyard,' said Stan the

Dog. 'And nobody here wants to know us.'

'Brace up!' cried Charlemagne. 'We're about to make our breakthrough! We're going straight to the top!' And he knocked on the door of the Archbishop's palace.

Now it so happened that the Archbishop himself was, at that very moment, in the hallway preparing to leave the palace, and so, when the servant opened the door, the Archbishop saw the cock and the dog standing there on the step.

'Your Highness!' said Charlemagne, bowing low to the servant. 'Allow me to introduce to you the Most Amazing Prodigy Of All Time – Stanislav the Dog! He does tricks you or I would have thought impossible! They are, indeed, miracles of . . .'

'Clear off!' said the servant, who had been too astonished to speak for a moment. And he began to close the door.

But Charlemagne the Cock suddenly lost his temper.

'LISTEN TO ME!' he cried, and he flew at the servant with his spurs flying. Well, the servant was so surprised he fell over backwards, and Charlemagne the Cock landed on his chest and screamed: 'THIS DOG IS A GENIUS! HIS LIKE HAS NEVER BEEN SEEN OUTSIDE OUR FARMYARD! JUST GIVE HIM A CHANCE TO SHOW YOU!'

And Stan the Dog, who had nervously slunk into the hallway, started to do his trick where he bounced around on his tail, juggling precious china ornaments (which he grabbed off the sideboard as he bounced past) whilst barking a popular Farmyard Chorus that always used to go down particularly well with the pigs.

'My china!' screamed the Archbishop. 'Stop him at once!' And several of the Archbishop's servants threw themselves at Stan the Dog. But Stan bounced out of their way brilliantly, and grabbed the Archbishop's mitre and started to balance a rare old Ming vase on the top of it.

'Isn't he great?' shouted Charlemagne the Cock.

'Grab him!' screamed the Archbishop, and the servants grabbed Charlemagne.

'But look at the dog!' squawked the cock. 'Don't you see how great he is? Do you know anyone else who can juggle like that?'

But just then – as luck would have it – all the butlers and chambermaids and kitchen skivvies and gardeners, who had heard all the noise, came bursting into the Archbishop's hall. They stood there for a moment horrified, as they watched a barking dog, bouncing around on his tail, juggling the most precious pieces of the Archbishop's prize collection of china.

'Stop him!' roared the Archbishop again. And without more ado everybody descended on poor Stan, and he disappeared under a mound of flailing arms and legs. As a result, of course, all the Archbishop's best china crashed to the floor and was smashed into smithereens.

'Now look what you've done!' yelled Charlemagne.

'Now look what *we've* done!' exclaimed the Archbishop. 'Listen to me! You're both filthy, you look as if you slept in a hedge, you stink of the chamber-pot and you dare to burst into my palace and wreck my best china! Well! You're going to pay for it! Throw them into my darkest dungeons!'

And the Archbishop's servants were just about to do so, when suddenly a voice spoke from above them.

'Silence, everybody!' said the Voice.

Everybody froze. Then the Voice continued: 'Don't you know who this is? Archbishop! Shame on you! This is the Voice of God!'

The Archbishop fell to his knees, and muttered a prayer, and everyone else followed suit.

'That's better!' said the Voice of God. 'Now let Stan the Dog go free. He didn't mean no harm.'

So they let go of Stan the Dog.

'And now,' continued the Voice of God. 'Let Charlemagne the Cock go!'

So they let go of Charlemagne the Cock.

'Now shut your eyes and wait for me to tell you to open them again!' said the Voice of God.

So they all shut their eyes, and Stan the Dog and Charlemagne the Cock fled out of the Archbishop's palace as fast as their legs could carry them.

I don't know how long the Archbishop and his servants remained kneeling there with their eyes shut, but I am certain that the Voice of God never told them to open their eyes again. For, of course, the Voice wasn't the Voice of God at all – it was the Voice of Stan the Dog.

'You are, as I say, a very talented dog,' said Charlemagne as they ran down the road. 'But I'd almost forgotten you were a ventriloquist as well!'

'Luckily for us!' replied Stan. 'But look here, Charlemagne, I'll always be talented – it's just the way I am. Only I'd rather use those talents where they're appreciated, instead of where they get us into trouble.'

'Stanislav,' said Charlemagne, 'maybe you're right.'

And so the two friends returned to the farmyard. And Stanislav the Dog continued to perform his astounding tricks for the entertainment of the other farm animals, and they always loved him.

And even though Charlemagne occasionally

squawked a bit at night, and said that it was a waste of talent, Stan the Dog stayed where he was – happy to be the Star of the Farmyard.

The Improving Mirror

A magician once made a magical mirror that made everything look better than it really was.

It would make an ugly man look handsome, and a plain woman beautiful.

'I will bring happiness to a lot of people with this mirror,' said the Magician to himself. And he went to the main city, where he had his invention announced to the public. Naturally everybody was very curious to see themselves more handsome and more beautiful than they really were, and they queued up to see the magical improving mirror.

The Magician rubbed his hands and said: 'I will not only make people happy – I will also make my fortune!'

But before he was able to show the mirror to a single person, a most unlucky thing occurred.

It so happened that the King of that particular

country had married a Queen who was bad-tempered, selfish and cruel. The King put up with all her faults of character, however, because she was also very, very beautiful. She also happened to be extremely vain. So when she heard about the improving mirror, she simply couldn't wait to get her hands on it before anyone else.

'But, my dear,' said the King, 'you know you are already the most beautiful lady in the realm. And I should know – I searched the kingdom through and I found no one whose looks surpassed yours. That's why I married you.'

But the Queen replied: 'I must see how even more beautiful I can look in this magical mirror.' And nothing would satisfy her but to be the first to look in the improving mirror.

So the King sent for the Magician with strict instructions that he was to show the mirror to nobody until he had demonstrated it to Queen Pavona.

Well, the Magician entered the audience chamber with a feeling of dread.

'Great Queen!' he said with a low bow. 'You are the most peerless beauty in this land. No one could be more beautiful than you are now. I beg you not to look in my magic mirror!'

But the Queen could not contain her eagerness to see herself in the improving glass, and she said: 'Show me at once! I must see myself even more beautiful than I really am!'

'Alas!' said the Magician. 'I made this mirror

for those less fortunate in looks – to give them hope of how they might be.'

'Show me!' cried Queen Pavona. 'Or I will have you executed on the spot!'

Well, the poor Magician saw there was nothing for it but that he must show the Queen the magic improving mirror. So he brought out the special box in which he kept it locked away, but he did so with a heavy heart.

He took the key, which he had tied around his waist, and opened up the lock. The courtiers pressed around, but the King ordered them to stand back, and the box was brought nearer the throne.

Then the Magician lifted the lid, and the Queen peered in. There she saw the magic mirror – lying face down.

'Your Majesty!' said the Magician. 'I fear only evil will come of your looking in my magic mirror.'

'Silence!' shouted the Queen, and she seized the mirror and held it up to her face.

For some moments she did not speak, nor move, nor even breathe. She was so dazzled by the reflection before her. If her eyes had been dark and mysterious before, now they were two pools of midnight. If her cheeks had been fair and rosy before, now they were like snow touched by the dawn sun. And if her face had been well-shaped before, now it was so perfect that it would carry away the soul of anyone who gazed upon it.

For what seemed a lifetime, her eyes feasted on

the image before her. And everyone in the court waited with bated breath.

Eventually the King spoke: 'Well, my dear? what do you see?' he asked.

Slowly the Queen came to her senses. As she did so, the Magician trembled in his shoes, and humbled himself on the floor before her.

'Does it make you more beautiful?' asked the King.

Queen Pavona suddenly hid the mirror in her sleeve, glared around the court and cried: 'Of course not! It's just an ordinary mirror! Have this charlatan thrown into the darkest dungeon!'

So the poor Magician was carried off down to the darkest dungeon.

Meanwhile the King turned to Queen Pavona and said: 'Perhaps it will work for me, since I am less well-favoured than you.'

'I tell you it's just an ordinary mirror!' cried the Queen. 'I shall use it in my chamber.'

And with that, she went straight to her room, and hid the magic mirror in her great chest.

Now the truth of the matter is that the moment Queen Pavona had looked into the magic mirror and seen herself even more beautiful than she really was, she had been consumed with jealousy. She could not bear the thought that there was a beauty greater than hers – even though it was that of her own reflection! So she locked the mirror away, resolving that no one should ever look in it again.

None the less, she could not forget what she had seen in that looking-glass, and – despite her resolve – she found herself drawn to it, and time and again she would creep into her room and steal a look in the magic glass. Before long, she was spending many hours of the day alone in her chamber, gazing into that mirror, trying to see what made her reflection so much more beautiful than she already was.

As the weeks passed, Queen Pavona began to try and make herself more like her reflection in the magic looking-glass. But, of course, it was no use. For no matter how beautiful she made herself, her reflection became even more beautiful still.

The more she tried, the more she failed, and the more she failed to be as beautiful as her reflection in the magic mirror, the more time she spent alone in her room, gazing into it. Until eventually she hardly ever came out of her room – not even to eat or to dance or to make merry with the rest of the court.

Meanwhile the King grew more and more anxious about his wife, for she never explained to him what kept her in her room from morn till night, and whenever he entered the chamber, she always took care to hide the magic mirror.

One night, however, after Queen Pavona had been poring all day over her reflection in the fatal looking-glass, she fell asleep with it still in her hand.

It so happened that some time later the King entered her chamber to kiss her goodnight, as was his custom.

The King had, long ago, guessed that the magic mirror was the cause of his wife's strange behaviour, and he too had long been curious to see just what was so special about it. So when he found her fast asleep on her couch, with the magic mirror still in her hand, he couldn't resist. He lifted it slowly to her face and gazed into it. And there he saw for the first time his Queen's reflection in the magic looking-glass.

The King had believed he would never find another woman more beautiful to his sight than Queen Pavona. But now he saw in the magic mirror the reflection of someone who was three times as beautiful, and he let out a cry as if he had been stabbed to the heart.

At that, the Queen woke up with a scream of rage, and she struck the King with the mirror – so hard that he fell over.

'How dare you look in this mirror!' she cried, her face all screwed up with anger. Well, of course, when the King looked at her now with her face distorted by rage, he thought that Queen Pavona was almost ugly compared to her reflection.

'How dare you strike me!' cried the King. And he strode out of the Queen's chamber, resolving that he would put up with her ill-temper no longer.

From that day on, the King scarcely spoke to his Queen, or even set eyes on her. But he could not forget the vision of loveliness that he had seen in the magic glass.

Now all this while, the poor Magician had been languishing in the darkest dungeon. And every day he cursed himself for making the improving mirror.

Then one day, in the midst of his misery, the door of his cell was flung open and in strode the King!

The Magician fell at his feet and cried: 'Mercy, O King! Have you come to release me? You know I've done nothing wrong.'

'Well . . . that's as maybe,' replied the King. 'But if you want to get out of this dungeon, there is something you must do for me.'

'Anything that is within my power!' exclaimed the Magician.

'Very well,' said the King. 'I want you to change the Queen, my wife, for her reflection in your magic looking-glass.'

'But, Your Majesty!' cried the Magician. 'That would be a cruel thing to do to your wife!'

'I don't care!' replied the King. 'I am sick of her evil temper, her selfishness and her cruelty. And now I have seen her reflection – which is so much more beautiful than she ever can be – I am no longer even satisfied by her looks. Can you change her for her reflection?'

'Alas!' cried the Magician. 'Is this the only way I can gain my freedom?'

'If you can't do it, then you can rot in here until you die – for all I care!' said the King.

'Then I shall do it,' said the Magician. 'But we shall both suffer for it.'

And so the King released the Magician from his dungeon, and the Magician was led into the Queen's chamber.

The Queen was standing as usual in front of the magic glass, staring at her reflection. 'What do you want?' she cried as the King entered.

'You wish you were more like your reflection, my dear?' said the King. 'Then so do I!'

At which the Magician threw a handful of magic dust into the air, and for a few moments it filled the chamber so that no one could see. Then, as the dust cleared, a most extraordinary thing happened.

There was a flash and a groan, and suddenly the mirror rose up into the air – but the Queen's reflection stayed where it was! Then the mirror turned over several times in the air, before landing over the Queen herself.

And so the King had his wish.

From that time on, Queen Pavona's beautiful reflection became his wife, and the real queen was trapped for ever in the mirror. But, just as the Magician had promised, the King lived to regret the change. For even though she was now his wife, the Queen's reflection was still only a reflection, and – when the King tried to touch her beautiful skin – he found it was as cold as glass.

What's more, he soon discovered that the Queen's reflection was not only more beautiful than the real Queen, it was also more heartless, more selfish and even more ill-tempered. And many a time he longed for the Magician to change them back.

But the Magician had long since fled the country, and now lived in miserable exile, swearing that he would never make another magic mirror that could so inflame the vanity of those who were already vain enough.

The Mermaid Who Pitied a Sailor

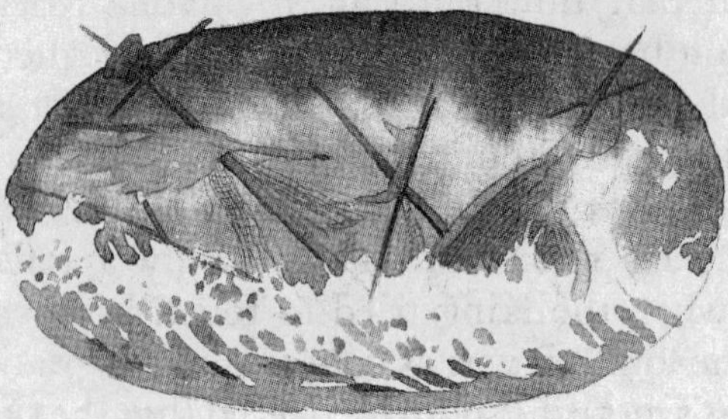

There was once a mermaid who pitied the sailors who drowned in the windy sea.

Her sisters would laugh whenever a ship foundered and sank, and they would swim down to steal the silver combs and golden goblets from the sunken vessels. But Varina, the mermaid, wept in her watery cave, thinking of the men who had lost their lives.

'What in the sea is the matter with you?' her sisters would exclaim. 'While we are finding jewels and silver, you sit alone and grieve. It's not our fault if their ships are wrecked! That is the way the sea goes. Besides, these sailors mean nothing to us, sister, for they are not of our kind.'

But Varina the mermaid replied: 'What though they are not of our kind? Their hopes are still hopes. Their lives are lives.'

And her sisters just laughed at her, and splashed her with their finny tails.

One day, however, a great ship struck the rocks near by and started to sink. All the other mermaids stayed sitting on the rocks where they had been singing, but Varina slipped away into the sea, and swam around and around the sinking ship, calling out to see if any sailors were still alive.

She saw the Boatswain in his chair, but he had drowned as the ship first took water. She saw the First Mate on the poop deck, but he had drowned, caught in the rigging. She saw the Captain, but he, too, was lifeless, with his hands around the wheel.

Then she heard a tap-tap-tapping, coming from the side of the sunken ship, and there was the frightened face of the Cabin Boy, peering through a crack.

'How are you still alive, when your ship-mates are all drowned?' asked Varina.

'I'm caught in a pocket of air,' replied the Cabin Boy. 'But it will not last, and we are now so deep at the bottom of the ocean, that unless I can swim as fast as a fish through the ship's hold, through the galley and up on to the deck, I shall drown long before I can make my way up to the waves above.'

'But I swim faster than forty fishes!' exclaimed the mermaid. And without more ado, she twitched her tail, and swam to the deck, and down through the galley and along through the ship's hold to the place where the Cabin Boy was trapped in the pocket of air.

Then she took his hand and said: 'Hold your

landlubberly breath!' And back she swam, faster than forty fishes, back through the ship's hold, back through the galley and up to the deck and then up and up and up to the waves above.

There the Cabin Boy got back his breath. But the moment he turned to the mermaid, it left his body again, for he suddenly saw how beautiful she was.

'Thank you!' he finally managed to say. 'Now I can swim to the shore.' But the mermaid would not let go of his hand.

'Come with me to my watery cave,' she said.

'Oh no!' cried the Cabin Boy. 'You have saved my life, and grateful I am more than six times seven, but I know you mermaids are not of our kind and bring us poor sailors only despair.'

But still the mermaid would not let go of his hand, and she swam as fast as forty fishes, back to her watery cave.

And there she gave the Cabin Boy sea-kelp and sargassum, bladder-wrack and sea-urchins, all served up on a silver dish. But the Cabin Boy looked pale as death and said:

'Your kindness overwhelms me, and grateful I am more than six times sixty, but you are not of my kind, and these ocean foods to me are thin and savourless. Let me go.'

But the mermaid wrapped him up in a seaweed bed and said: 'Sleep and tomorrow you may feel better.'

The Cabin Boy replied: 'You are kind beyond words, and grateful I am more than six times six

hundred, but I am not of your kind, and this bed is cold and damp, and my blood runs as chill as sea-water in my veins.'

Finally the mermaid said to the Cabin Boy: 'Shut your eyes, and I shall sing you a song that will make you forget your sorrow.'

But at that, the Cabin Boy leapt out of the bed and cried: 'Oh no! That you must not! For don't you know it is your mermaids' singing that lulls our senses and lures us poor sailors on to the rocks so that we founder and drown?'

When the mermaid heard this, she was truly astonished. She swam to her sisters and cried out: 'Sisters! Throw away those silver combs and throw away those golden goblets that we have stolen from the drowned sailors – for it is our songs that lull these sailors' senses and lure them on to the rocks.'

When they heard this, the mermaids all wept salty tears for the lives of the men who had been drowned through their songs. And from that day on the mermaids resolved to sit on the rocks and sing only when they were sure there was no ship in sight.

As for Varina, she swam back to her watery cave, and there she found the Cabin Boy still waiting for her.

'I could not leave,' he said taking her hand. 'For though we are of different kind, where shall I find such goodness of heart as yours?'

And there and then he took the mermaid in his

arms and kissed her, and she wrapped her finny tail around him, and they both fell into the sea.

Then they swam as if they were one creature instead of two – fast as forty fishes – until, at last, they reached the land the Cabin Boy had left, many years before. And there they fell asleep upon the shore – exhausted and sea-worn.

When the Cabin Boy awoke, he looked and he found Varina still asleep beside him. And as he stared at her, all the breath once again went from his body, for her finny tail had disappeared, and there she lay beside him – no longer a mermaid, but a beautiful girl, who opened her eyes and looked at him not with pity but with love.

Forget-Me-Nuts

A long, long time ago in a very distant land, there once lived a king with a very bad conscience. But he didn't let his conscience trouble him one little bit, because in that land there also happened to grow a very rare and peculiar fruit. It was known as the forget-me-nut. And whenever King Yorick felt bad about something he'd done, or something he hadn't done, he would chew a forget-me-nut, and whatever it was that was worrying him would simply vanish from his mind.

One cold winter's day, for example, King Yorick was being carried home to his palace in his specially heated chair, when he noticed a poor man dressed in rags with his wife and three small children shivering under a wall.

'Oh dear,' said King Yorick, when he got back to his palace. 'I really ought to do something about all the poor people who have nowhere to live in this bitter cold weather. I suppose I ought to convert one of my palaces into a home for them . . .'

'Oh! But, Your Majesty!' said his Chancellor. 'You've only got sixteen palaces! If you were to lose one of them, you'd have one less than King Fancypants of Swaggerland – and that wouldn't do, would it?'

'Good gracious no! That wouldn't do at all,' replied King Yorick.

'Best go to bed and chew one of those delightful forget-me-nuts,' said his Chancellor.

'Yes, perhaps you're right,' sighed King Yorick.

So he put himself to bed with a hot-water bottle, chewed a forget-me-nut, and had soon forgotten all about the poor family, who were freezing outside in the ice and snow.

But, of course, the poor man and his family outside didn't have any forget-me-nuts to chew on. Forget-me-nuts were worth their weight in gold – far too rare and expensive for the likes of them.

And even if they could have found one, it wouldn't have done them any good, for, you see, forget-me-nuts only helped you to forget your conscience – they didn't help you to forget that you were cold or hungry or homeless.

As a matter of fact, the forget-me-nuts didn't really help King Yorick that much either, for even though he chewed on one most days – and sometimes two or three – he was always pretty miserable, though he never quite knew why.

'Perhaps if I had another palace built so I had

one *more* than King Fancypants of Swaggerland – I'd feel happier?' said King Yorick.

'Exactly so,' said the Lord Chancellor (whose brother got all the building contracts).

And so King Yorick had yet another palace built. It was opened with great celebrations and fantastic fireworks and a lavish feast that went on for three whole days. Then the new palace stood empty for the rest of the year like all the other palaces.

Now the poor man, whose family the King had seen shivering in the midst of winter, had a son whose name was Tim. And one day, Tim said to his father: 'Father! I cannot bear to see you so unhappy! I'm going to bring King Yorick to his senses!'

Whereupon Tim's father exclaimed: 'But what on earth can you do, Tim? You're so small.'

'You'll see!' said Tim. And there and then he set off for the King's palace.

When he reached it, he found the doors shut tight against the freezing winter and the walls too high to climb.

'What *am* I going to do?' thought Tim to himself. 'I'll never even get into the palace – let alone bring the King to his senses!'

But he didn't give up. He sat on a stone outside the palace and waited to see what would happen. And as he sat there, the sky grew dark and the world grew quiet, as if it too were waiting to see what would happen. Then finally it started to snow. And the snow fell on Tim's head and

shoulders. But still he just sat there, watching the King's palace.

Well, after a while, Tim saw a face at one of the windows. And all the while the snow fell thicker and faster, until it quite covered Tim's head and his shoulders. Yet still Tim just sat and waited to see what would happen.

Before long, the window opened, and a boy stuck his head out and called to Tim: 'Aren't you cold?'

Now Tim was so used to being cold that he scarcely thought about it any more. But, now he came to think about it, he realized he was so cold he couldn't even speak.

'You'd better come in and get warm,' said the boy at the window.

But Tim found he could neither speak nor move. He was frozen fast and completely covered in snow like a snowman.

So the boy climbed out of the window, brushed the snow off Tim, and lifted him in through the

window. (For, truth to tell, Tim was extremely small and light because he'd never really had enough to eat all his life.)

Well, it didn't take Tim long to thaw out and explain what he was doing.

'That's odd!' replied the boy. 'I was wondering what I could do to make *my* father happier too.'

'But your father's the king!' exclaimed Tim, who had already guessed that the boy was King Yorick's son. 'He must have everything he could ever want!'

'That's right,' replied the Prince. 'But he's miserable from morn till night. I try and cheer him up, but he doesn't even seem to notice I exist. He just sits and chews forget-me-nuts.'

When Tim heard this, he sat and stared into the fire.

'How on earth are we going to help our fathers to be happier?' he said.

No sooner had he spoken these words than a most extraordinary thing happened. The fire began to move, and, as the two boys watched, the red-hot coals turned over and around until they formed themselves into a face that spoke and said: 'The Key of Memory is the only thing that will bring your fathers happiness. But be warned – it will also bring grief as well.'

'Where do we find the Key of Memory?' asked Tim.

'Go with your consciences . . .' replied the fire.

'What?' said the Prince.

'What?' said Tim.

But the coals in the fire shifted around again, and didn't say another word.

Then suddenly there was a noise like thunder. Tim and the Prince rushed to the window and looked out into the freezing black night. They could see two points of light coming towards them fast.

'What d'you think they are?' asked Tim.

'Perhaps they're our consciences,' said the Prince.

'Don't be daft!' said Tim.

And the two points of light got nearer and nearer, until suddenly two huge black stallions, breathing fire out of their nostrils, burst out of the night, leapt over the palace wall, and reared up to a halt underneath the window.

Tim looked at the Prince, and the Prince looked at Tim, and Tim shrugged and said: 'Well, I don't know . . . maybe you're right . . .' And without another word they leapt on to the backs of those stallions and galloped off into the night.

The next morning, when King Yorick found that his son had vanished, he wrung his hands in despair. 'What shall I do? My only son has run away . . . I should have loved him more! I should have been a better father!'

'Don't make such a fuss!' said his Chancellor. 'Just chew a forget-me-nut, and you'll soon feel better.'

So the King ate a forget-me-nut, and, after a while, he forgot all about it. But when he went to bed that night, he found the Queen crying into her pillow.

'What on earth's the matter with you?' he asked.

The Queen looked at him in anger and exclaimed: 'What! Have you already forgotten that our son has run away?'

'Oh, don't make such a fuss,' said the King. 'Have a forget-me-nut.' And he offered the bowl of nuts to the Queen, but she seized it from his grasp and threw the entire thing on the fire.

'Don't!' cried the King. 'Those are worth their weight in gold!' But it was too late. The nuts burst into flame, and the smoke went up the chimney.

Meanwhile, Tim and the Prince were riding through the frozen Northlands on the backs of their fire-breathing stallions.

By and by, they saw a cloud on the horizon, and the stallions redoubled their speed. And, by and by, they reached the cloud and found it was a pall of smoke, under which their stallions came to a halt. When Tim and the Prince looked down, they saw they were on the edge of a sheer cliff that dropped straight down a thousand feet into a lake of fire.

But they didn't have time to be frightened, for – to their horror – their stallions reared up, pawed the air, and then leapt straight off the cliff and plunged down towards the fiery lake.

The two boys shut their eyes, convinced that their last moment had come, but, as they reached the surface of the burning lake and they felt the fire licking up around their stallions' bellies, suddenly the flames seemed to separate, and they found themselves plummeting down into a black hole until they disappeared below the surface of the lake of fire.

For a moment, their eyes were filled with smoke, and they couldn't see a thing, but when they opened them again, they found they had landed in a vast cavern. And there in the centre of the cavern was a great forge, with flames shooting up and feeding the fiery lake above. At the forge worked a huge blacksmith, with iron bands on his arms and fire coming from his nostrils.

The two stallions reared in the air once more, and Tim and the Prince fell off onto a pile of straw.

When he saw them, the huge blacksmith stopped his work and laughed. And every time he laughed, the flames shot out from his nostrils and set fire to his beard, so he had to keep running to the water-butt to put it out.

Meanwhile Tim had got to his feet and said:

'We have come for the Key of Memory.'

'Have you now?' roared the blacksmith, and this time he laughed so hard that he set fire to his hood, and he had to plunge his whole head into the water-butt.

'We've been told it is the only thing that will bring our fathers happiness,' said the Prince.

'And grief!' roared the blacksmith, and he laughed again so long and loud that he set fire to his jerkin, and he had to jump into the water-butt right up to his neck.

'Is the Key of Memory here?' asked Tim.

The blacksmith lay there, half in the water, and roared: 'I've just finished making it! It's on the anvil.'

The two boys turned and saw a huge key lying on the anvil and glowing red-hot.

'Take a pair of tongs,' said the blacksmith, 'and drop it in this water butt.'

So the Prince took a long pair of tongs, lifted up the red-hot key and dropped it into the water-butt, where the giant blacksmith was still sitting. Immediately the blacksmith disappeared in a cloud of steam, and when the steam had cleared away, the blacksmith had gone, and there was an old woman, whose face was red like the coals of the fire. The old woman turned to the Prince and said:

'Prince! In the unhappiest part of your father's kingdom, you will find a chest filled with your father's memories. This is the only key that will unlock it.'

Then the old woman seemed to fall into pieces,

and sank like glowing embers down into the water-butt.

So Tim and the Prince took the key, and looked for their black stallions, but they had disappeared too.

'Well,' said Tim. 'It looks as if we've got to walk home.'

The two boys searched until eventually they found the entrance to the cavern, and they were able to climb up and escape. When they reached the world above, however, they found that the lake of fire was just an ordinary lake. And there at the water's edge were two grey horses – just ordinary horses.

They rode back through the frozen Northlands, but what had taken a few minutes on the marvellous stallions now took days. And what had taken hours now took weeks.

But eventually they arrived back in the land of King Yorick.

'Where shall we find the unhappiest part of my father's kingdom?' asked the Prince.

'I know where that is!' said Tim, and he led the Prince to the place where forty beggars slept under a bridge, but they couldn't find the chest there.

Then Tim led the Prince to a shed, where twenty robbers were hiding for fear of being caught. But they didn't find the chest there.

Finally Tim led the Prince to the place where his own mother and father and brother and sister were huddled around a poor fire, beneath the wall. But when they saw Tim, their faces burst into smiles of happiness, and they didn't find the chest there.

'Well, it beats me,' said Tim. 'I don't know where else to look.'

So the Prince returned to the palace, and Tim went with him. There they found the King sitting under a nutmeg tree with tears in his eyes.

The Prince stood in front of his father, and said: 'What is the matter? You're the King! You have seventeen palaces and everything your heart could desire! Why are you unhappy?'

The King looked at his son without recognizing him and said: 'I forgot to love my son, and he ran away. And now I've even forgotten what he looks like!'

At that moment, Tim noticed that the King was sitting on a rusty old iron chest. He handed the key to the Prince and the Prince tried it in the lock. It fitted exactly.

'Father,' said the Prince. 'I've come back in hopes to bring you happiness.'

With that, he unlocked the chest, and at once the lid flew open and a million black thoughts flew into the air and blotted out the sun for a moment.

The King gave a roar of grief, as the black cloud suddenly melted into his mind, and he looked into the Prince's eyes and said:

'My son, I fear this is not happiness you have brought me, for I now remember everyone who has gone hungry – even for a day. I now remember every poor mother who cannot feed her children.

I now remember every poor father who cannot clothe his family nor provide a roof to keep the rain and snow from their heads. I now remember everyone whose sufferings I have ignored, and my heart is overcome with grief.'

'But, Your Majesty!' cried Tim. 'Why don't you give up just one of your seventeen palaces to house the hungry?'

King Yorick looked at Tim and, for the first time in years, he smiled: 'I'll do better than that!' he said.

And then and there King Yorick became the first king to give up living in a palace. Instead he lived in a comfortable house, that was just roomy enough for himself and his family and also for Tim and his mother and father and brother and sister. King Yorick opened up every one of his seventeen palaces so that from that day on there was not one single homeless person in the kingdom.

The Lord Chancellor left in disgust, and went to work with King Fancypants of Swaggerland. And so did the Chancellor's brother.

Then King Yorick ordered his gardeners to cut down all the orchards of forget-me-nut trees. This they did. And from that day on everyone forgot that there was ever such a thing as a forget-me-nut.

Eyes-All-Over

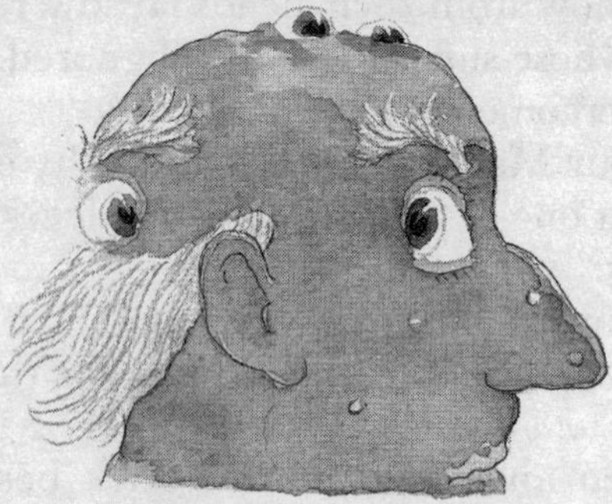

There was once an old man whose name was Eyes-All-Over, because that's what he had. He had eyes in the back of his head, eyes on the top of his head, eyes on his elbows, and eyes on his knees. He even had one eye on the bottom of each foot.

'Nobody ever catches me out!' chuckled old Eyes-All-Over. And it was true, because each of his eyes could see different things.

The eyes in the back of his head could see things that happened yesterday. The eyes on the top of his head could see things that happened a long way away. The eyes on his elbows could see everyone else's mistakes. The eyes on his knees could see everyone else's hopes. And the eyes on the soles of his feet could see things that would never happen.

Now the only thing in the whole world that old

Eyes-All-Over really cared for was a pot of gold that he kept under the floorboards in his bedroom. Every night he would close all the shutters, draw the curtains, take out his pot of gold and count it – just to make sure it was all there.

And as he counted it, the eyes on the top of his head looked around to make sure no one was peeping in – while the eyes in the back of his head made sure the coins were the same as they were yesterday.

Every week his pot of gold would get larger, because, whenever he went to market, the eyes in his elbows spotted everyone else's mistakes – so, if someone were selling a pig for a pound that was really worth three, old Eyes-All-Over would snap it up and sell it again as quick as fat in the frying-pan!

And, of course, old Eyes-All-Over never warned anybody they were making a mistake or that they'd lose their money. Oh no! He was far too busy thinking about adding all those golden guineas to his pot of gold.

Well, one day, Eyes-All-Over was sitting at home, counting through his pot of gold as usual, when suddenly there was a knock on the door.

'Burglars!' he exclaimed to himself. Then he thought: 'No . . . wait a minute . . . burglars wouldn't knock on the door. They'd just climb down the chimney.'

So he carefully hid away his pot of gold, and then he opened the door – just a crack.

There on the step stood a thin girl who said: 'I'm hungry and I have nowhere to live. May I do some work for you to earn a slice of bread and dripping?'

'Bread and dripping!' exclaimed old Eyes-All-Over. 'D'you think I'm made of money?'

'I could clean your house or chop your wood for you,' said the girl.

'Listen!' said Eyes-All-Over. 'The eyes in my knees can see what you're hoping – you're hoping to be rich one day and live in a nice house like this! Why, you'd probably cut my throat while I'm asleep! Be off with you!'

'Oh no!' said the poor girl. 'I'd never do a thing like that!'

Well, old Eyes-All-Over slyly slipped off a shoe and looked at the girl with one of the eyes in the soles of his feet – the eyes that could see things that would never happen. He saw at once that she would never do anything to harm anyone.

'Hmm! Very well,' he said. 'I do need some firewood chopping.'

So the girl chopped some firewood, and he gave her a piece of bread (without any dripping) and let her sleep that night in the woodshed.

The next day, old Eyes-All-Over woke up to find his house clean and neat and a breakfast of beans and ham waiting for him on the table. For the girl (whose name was May) had been up working hard for several hours already.

So Eyes-All-Over gave her another piece of dry bread and said: 'You can stay another day.'

Well, May stayed and worked for old Eyes-All-Over for some years. In return he let her sleep in the woodshed and allowed her to eat one piece of bread in the morning and one bowl of soup at night. 'Eh, eh!' he used to grin to himself. 'She costs me nothing and she works as hard as six men. What a bargain!'

One day, however, a stranger was riding past the house, when he caught sight of May digging the cabbage patch. She was still dressed in the same rags she'd been wearing when she first arrived (for it never occurred to old Eyes-All-Over that she might need new clothes) and she was exhausted from all her hard work, but even so May looked so beautiful that the young man fell in love with her on the spot. And, not long after, she fell in love with him.

So the young man went to Eyes-All-Over and told him that he wanted to marry May.

Now old Eyes-All-Over saw at once that he must be a rich young fellow. 'Eh, eh!' he thought, 'I can make a good bargain out of this business!'

But he put on a sad face and said: 'Oh no! You can't take young May away from me! She cooks my breakfast every morning!'

'Very well,' said the young man, 'take this.' And he handed old Eyes-All-Over a ruby ring. 'With that you can hire the finest cook in the world to make your breakfast every day!'

But old Eyes-All-Over slyly looked at the young man with the eyes in the back of his head – the eyes that could see things that had happened

yesterday – and he could see that only yesterday the young man had bought a fine fur coat. So old Eyes-All-Over screwed up his face and looked very sad and said: 'Oh, young sir, you don't really mean to take young May away from me? Don't you know she cuts my wood every day and makes my fire . . . I'd need a fine fur coat to keep me warm, if you were to take her away from me.'

So the young man went and fetched the fine fur coat, which he had actually bought for his father, and gave it to old Eyes-All-Over.

'There,' he said. 'Now may I marry May?'

But old Eyes-All-Over looked with the eyes on the top of his head – the eyes that could see things that were happening far away – and he could see that the young man's father, who was waiting for his return, lived in a fine palace, surrounded by fabulous wealth.

So Eyes-All-Over took out his hanky, and pretended to cry salty tears into it.

'Oh, good sir!' he said. 'You cannot possibly want to take young May away from me! She works so hard and keeps my house so neat and clean. Why! She's worth her weight in gold!'

So the young man rode off and returned, some time later, with a chest filled with gold pieces that altogether weighed exactly the same as young May.

'Now,' he said, 'May and I must go and be married.'

But old Eyes-All-Over hadn't finished yet. 'I can still screw even more out of this bargain!' he said to himself. Then he looked at the young man with the eyes in his knees – the eyes that could see people's hopes – and he could see that the young man had hopes, one day, to be a king – for he was, in fact, a prince.

So old Eyes-All-Over clutched his heart and said: 'Ah! Good sir! Would you take this child from me? She has been like a daughter to me these many years. I would not part with her for half a kingdom!'

'Very well,' said the Prince, and there and then he signed away half his kingdom to old Eyes-All-Over. Then he lifted May up on to his horse, and they rode off together – to be married with great feasting and merry-making in his father's palace.

As they rode away, old Eyes-All-Over rubbed his hands with glee.

'What a bargain!' he said to himself. 'I get all those years of work out of that thin stick of a girl, and then I sell her off for jewels and furs and gold and half a kingdom! I certainly am the sharpest chap around!'

But, at that very moment, he looked at himself with the eyes in his elbows – the eyes that saw people's mistakes – and he saw, to his horror, that he himself had made a big mistake, though he didn't know what.

As he got his lonely breakfast, however, and sat by his lonely fire, he began to realize what it was, for he found himself longing to hear May's voice singing in the garden and to see her face across the room. Soon he found himself thinking that he would give back everything just to have May give him one of her smiles.

But, when he looked at himself with the eyes in the soles of his feet – the eyes that saw things that would never happen – he knew she would never smile at him again.

And this time, old Eyes-All-Over cried real tears, for he suddenly realized that – when he gave May away – he'd given away the only thing he'd ever really loved.

And he cursed himself that – all the time she'd lived with him – he'd given her nothing but hard words and hard work, and had never given her any reason to care for him.

And old Eyes-All-Over then saw – clearer than anything he'd ever seen in his life – that despite having eyes all over, he had really been quite, quite blind.

The Snow Baby

An old woman once wished she had a child. But she never married, and now she lived all alone in a bare cottage beside a dark wood.

One day, however, around Christmas time, when the sky was yellow and heavy with snow, she looked out of the little window by her bed, and thought she saw the evening star.

'That's strange,' she said to herself, 'to see the evening star on such a stormy night. It must be a lucky star.'

So there and then she made a wish. I can't tell you what she wished for, because she never told anyone, but I think I can guess – can't you?

Now, as it happened, the light that the old woman had seen was not the evening star – in fact it was not a star at all, but a firefly. The firefly overheard the old lady's wish, and felt very sorry for her. So it flew to the place where all fireflies go to fetch their lights, and told its comrades what it had heard. And they all agreed to try and help her.

Well that night it began to snow from the black sky on to the black ground, until – as if by magic – the ground turned white, and the morning broke over a different world.

The old woman woke up and put on her shawl. Then she took a shovel and cleared away the snow from her door.

When she looked at the pile of snow she'd made, she smiled to herself and said: 'I don't think the evening star has granted my wish – so I'll make myself my own baby.'

And she spent the morning making the pile of snow into a snow baby.

That night, she sat in her cottage and felt very lonely. So she went to the door, and looked out at her snow baby.

'Tomorrow is Christmas Day,' she said to her snow baby. 'And here am I all alone in the world, and nobody cares whether I'm alive or dead – except you. And you'll be gonc when the snows thaw.'

Then she climbed into her bed, and put out her candle.

A moment later she woke up and looked out of her window. She could hear a sound like tiny bells jingling far, far away, and she could see a strange yellow light all around her cottage. She could not see, but above her all the fireflies in the world were gathered together on her roof. The last one had just arrived, and now they all flew together to form one single ball of light.

The next moment, the old woman couldn't believe her eyes as she watched a glowing ball of light descend on to the heap of snow that she had shaped like a baby. The light landed where the baby's heart would be. Then it poured into the snow baby and filled it top to toe!

The instant it did, the snow baby opened its eyes and looked around.

'What are you doing out there in the cold?' said the old woman. 'Come in at once.'

So the snow baby stepped unsteadily down from its little mound, and toddled towards the cottage door.

The old woman rushed to the door, flung it open and lifted her snow baby up in her arms. She kissed it and held it tight.

'Now,' she said, 'I will not be alone this Christmas.'

Then she tucked the snow baby up in her own bed, and bustled about the cottage to make everything ready.

The next morning the snow baby awoke to find a stocking hanging at the end of the bed.

'You must look in your stocking and see what St Nicholas has brought you,' said the old woman.

So the snow baby opened its stocking. Inside there was a chocolate medal, a wooden man on a trapeze, an old doll with one eye missing, a mince pie and an apple in the toe.

When the snow baby had opened all its presents and played with its toys, the old woman said: 'Now we must have our breakfast.'

So she sat her snow child on the other side of

the table, and they both ate a little toast and drank a little warm milk.

Just then they heard the church bell sounding across the snow. 'Now,' said the old woman, 'it's time we went to church.'

So she dressed the snow baby up in a woollen hat and muffler and a knitted woollen coat, and off they went, through the snow to the little church on the hill.

No one noticed the old woman and her snow baby, as they slipped into the back of the church while everyone else was on their knees. The two of them sat close together in the very back pew, holding hands. When the moment came, they stood up and sang the carols. Then, before the end of the service, they stole out again, before anyone else saw them.

Then the old woman and her snow baby ran back through the snow, laughing and shouting and throwing snowballs at each other.

When they finally got back to the cottage, there was a good smell coming from the old woman's oven.

'Now we must eat our Christmas pudding and mince pies,' said the old woman. 'I'm afraid I haven't got a goose or a ham pie to offer you.'

But the snow baby didn't seem to mind at all. They both sat down and ate the happiest Christmas dinner that the old woman could remember since she was a child.

As they finished, night began to fall, and the snow

baby grew tired, and the light with which it was filled grew dimmer – for the truth is that the fireflies needed to fetch new lights.

The old woman looked rather sadly at her snow baby.

'Must you go?' she asked. And the snow baby nodded. 'Well, thank you for keeping me company this Christmas,' said the old woman. 'I wish it could have gone on longer . . . but there it is . . .'

And then the first wonderful thing happened. The snow baby got up from its chair and came across to the old woman and kissed her.

And then the second wonderful thing happened. It spoke. 'Goodbye,' it said. Then it went out of the door, and the old woman watched from her window, as the snow baby climbed back on to its little mound of snow. Then the fireflies came out, one by one, and flew off dimly into the night to fetch new lights.

And the old woman fell asleep, nodding to herself as she remembered all the things she'd done that Christmas Day with her snow baby.

The next day, the sun shone, and the snows had gone. The old woman lit a fire and bustled about her little cottage. And when she felt brave enough, she went out of her door, and swept away the last heap of snow that had been – for a short time – her very own snow baby.

How the Badger Got Its Stripes

In the great long-ago, the badger was pure white all over.

'How sorry I feel for the Bear with his dull brown coat,' the Badger would say. 'And who would want to be like Leopard – all covered in spots? Or – worse still – like Tiger, with his vulgar striped coat! I am glad that the Maker Of All Things gave me this pure white coat without a blemish on it!'

This is how the Badger would boast as he paraded through the forest, until all the other creatures were thoroughly sick and tired of him.

'He always looks down his nose at me,' said the Rabbit, 'because only my tail is white.'

'And he sneers at me,' said the Field Mouse, 'because I'm such a mousy colour.'

'And he calls me an eye-sore!' exclaimed the Zebra.

'It's time we put a stop to it,' they said.

'Then may I make a suggestion?' asked the Fox, and he outlined a plan to which all the other animals agreed.

Some time later, the Fox went to the Badger and said:

'O Badger, please help us! You are, without doubt, the best-looking creature in the Wild Wood. It's not just your coat (which is exceedingly beautiful and without a blemish) but it is also . . . oh . . . the way you walk on your hind legs . . . the way you hold your head up . . . your superb manners and graceful ways . . . Won't you help us humbler animals by giving us lessons in how to improve our looks and how to carry ourselves?'

Well, the Badger was thrilled to hear all these compliments and he replied very graciously: 'Of course, my dear Fox. I'll see what I can do.'

So the Fox called all the animals to meet in the Great Glade, and said to them: 'Badger, here, has kindly agreed to give us lessons in how to look as handsome as he does. He will also instruct us in etiquette, deportment and fashion.'

There were one or two sniggers amongst the smaller animals at this point, but the Badger didn't notice. He stood up on his hind legs, puffed himself up with pride, and said: 'I am very happy to be in a position to help you less fortunate animals, and I must say I can see much room for improvement. You, Wolf, for example, have such a shabby coat . . .'

'But it's the only one I've got!' said the Wolf.

'And I pity you, Beaver,' went on the Badger,

'such an ordinary pelt you have . . . and as for that ridiculous tail . . .'

'Er, Badger,' interrupted the Fox, 'rather than going through all our short-comings (interesting and instructive though that certainly may be), why don't you teach us how to walk with our noses in the air – the way that makes you look so distinguished and sets off your beautiful unblemished white coat so well?'

'By all means,' said the Badger.

'Why not walk to the other end of the Glade, so we can see?' said the Fox.

'Certainly,' said the Badger. And so, without suspecting a thing, he started to walk to the other end of the Glade.

Now if the Badger had not been so blinded by his own self-satisfaction, he might have noticed the Rat and the Stoat and the Weasel smirking behind their paws. And if he had looked a little closer, he might have noticed a twinkle in many an animal's eye. But he didn't. He just swaggered along on his hind legs with his nose right up in the air, saying:

'This is the way to walk . . . notice how gracefully I raise my back legs . . . and see how I am always careful to keep my brush well oooooooooaaaarrrgggghhhup!'

This is the moment that the Badger discovered the Fox's plan. The Fox had got all the other animals to dig a deep pit at one end of the Great Glade. This they had filled with muddy water and madder-root, and then covered it over with branches and fern.

The Badger, with his nose in the air, had, of course, walked straight into it – feet first. And he sank in – right up to his neck.

'Help!' he cried. 'Help! My beautiful white coat! Please pull me out someone! Help!'

Well, of course, all the animals in the Glade laughed and pointed at the poor Badger, as he struggled to keep his head out of the muck. Eventually he had to pull himself out by his own efforts.

When the Badger looked down at his beautiful white coat, stained with mud and madder-root, he was so mortified that he ran off out of the forest with a pitiful howl. And he ran and he ran until he came to a lake of crystal water.

There he tried to clean the stuff off his coat, but madder-root is a powerful dye, and no matter what he did, he could not get it off.

'What shall I do?' he moaned to himself. 'My beautiful white coat . . . my pride and joy . . . ruined for ever! How can I hold my head up in the forest again?'

To makc matters worse, at that moment, a creature whom the Badger had never seen before swam up to him and said: 'What are you doing – washing your filthy old coat in our crystal-clear lake? Push off!'

The badger was speechless – not only because he wasn't used to being spoken to like this, but also because the creature had such a beautiful coat. It was as white and unblemished as the Badger's own coat used to be.

'Who are you?' asked the Badger.

'I'm Swan of course,' replied the Swan. 'Now shove off! We don't want dirty creatures like you around here!' And the Swan rose up on its legs and beat its powerful wings, and the Badger slunk away on all fours, with his tail between his legs.

For the rest of that day, the Badger hid himself away in a grove overlooking the crystal lake. From there he gazed down at the white Swan, gliding proudly about the lake, and the Badger was so filled with bitterness and envy that he thought he would burst.

That very night, however, he stole down to the Swan's nest, when the Swan was fast asleep, and very, very gently, he pulled out one of the Swan's feathers and then scuttled back to his hiding-place.

He did the same thing the next night, and the next and the next, and each night he returned to the grove, where he was busy making himself a new coat of white feathers, to cover up his stained fur.

And, because the Badger did all this so slowly and slyly, the Swan never noticed, until all but one of his feathers had disappeared.

That night the Swan couldn't sleep, because of the draught from where his feathers were missing, and so it was that he saw the Badger creeping up to steal the last one. As he did so the Swan rose up with a terrible cry. He pecked off the Badger's tail and beat him with his wings and chased him off.

Then the Swan returned to the crystal lake, and sat there lamenting over his lost feathers.

When the Maker Of All Things found the Swan – that he had made so beautiful – sitting there bald and featherless, he was extremely surprised.

But he was even more surprised when he went to the Wild Wood, and found the Badger parading about, looking quite ridiculous in his stolen feather coat!

'Badger!' exclaimed the Maker Of All Things. 'I knew you were vain, but I didn't know you were a thief as well!'

And there and then he took the feathers and gave them back to the Swan.

'From this day on,' he said to the Badger, 'you will wear only your coat stained with madder-root. And, if you're going to steal, I'd better give you a thief's mask as well!'

And the Maker Of All Things drew his fingers across the Badger's eyes, and left him with two black stripes – like a mask – from ears to snout.

The Badger was so ashamed that he ran off and hid, and to this very day all badgers avoid company. They live in solitude, stealing a little bit here and there, wherever they can. And each and every badger still wears a mask of stripes across its eyes.